Don't Touch My Shoes, Bruh!

written by E.G. Sparer AKA Ms. Ellen
illustrated by Luke Valentine

1st in the series of Ms. Ellen's Got Swag!

copyright©2017 By E.G. Sparer

Kymani just turned 10, and for his

birthday he got the best present ever. A pair of

Triple J's the best kicks ever made. They

were super dope and he was going to take

extra good care of them. No dirt on these

beauties.

It's not even my birthday!

Kymani got up extra early today; he

couldn't wait to show his friends his fresh

kicks. He wanted to be just like his cousin

Brandon who is a total sneakerhead. Yo, that

dude is always rockin' fresh sneaks!

AS he started heading to school, he

walked way back on his heels like a robot. He

had to be very careful not to step on the grass

or in a puddle.

As Kymani was rounding the corner, the neighbor's dog came over and sniffed his shoes. Kymani looked down at the dog.

"Hey! Don't touch my shoes, bruh!"

The dog looked up at Kymani and said,

"NO! YOU don't touch my shoes, bruh!"

The dog showed Kymani his little kicks.

"Huh?" said Kymani.

He wondered where the dog got those fresh shoes. Oh well.

Kymani continued on his way feeling anxious and excited. He knew he looked super fly. Just then a mama duck and her baby ducklings came waddling over. They came right up to Kymani's shoes.

"Hey! Don't touch my shoes, bruh!" said Kymani.

"No," said Mama Duck. "Don't touch OUR shoes, bruh!"

The mama duck and all her ducklings had little shoes on. They gave Kymani a look and waddled away.

"What the...?" said Kymani.

Kymani kept walking to school when along came a cat. Oh no, not again! The cat came right up to him and walked across his shoes.

"Hey! Don't touch my shoes, bruh!" said Kymani. The cat gave him a sassy look.

"No! YOU don't touch my shoes, bruh!" and the cat pointed to her cool shoes.

"This is crazy," thought Kymani as he started walking faster. "I gotta get to school!"

Just then an old lady came walking up the side walk; she stopped and looked down at Kymani's shoes.

"Wow," she said, bending down to touch them.

"Hey! Don't touch my shoes, bruh!" said Kymani.

The old lady looked at Kymani, pulled his ear and said, "No! Don't touch my shoes, bruh!"

She held up her old lady shoes and pointed to them.

"Oh, sorry, lady," said Kymani.

"Yikes," he thought. "I gotta get to school!" and started to run.

Kymani was almost there when he saw a girl in his class named Ja-Miracle walking towards him.

"Wow, you're so beautiful!" Kymani said.

"Huh?" she said. "Thank you."

"No!" Kymani said. "I wasn't talking to you" He pointed to his kicks. "I was talking to these beauties.

"HHHHHUMMMMFFFF!" Ja-Miracle said and ran off.

Finally, Kymani got to school; he looked down at his shoes.

"B-E-A-U-T-I-F-U-L," he thought.

But where was everyone? Kymani looked over by the oak tree and saw all his friends crowded in a circle looking at something.

"Hey guys," he yelled. "Come feast your eyes on my new Triple J's!"

One boy turned around, "Triple J's, dude? Those are old school. This girl's got Quadruple J's!"

There stood Ja-Miracle in the middle of the crowd; everyone was admiring her new kicks.

"What?!" said Kymani. "Let me see those!" He went to touch them.

Ja-Miracle looked at Kymani with a sly grin.

"Hey! Dont touch my shoes, bruh!"

Dedicated to Samantha, AJ and
especially Erica who is always there
for me! <3
And a big thanks to Luke Valentine.

Ellen Sparer's Big Plans;

Ellen Sparer's BIG PLANS are to make Ms. Ellen's Got Swag a household name, bridge the diversity gap in childrens' literature and continue to make kids laugh all around the world.

Luke Valentine's Big Plans;

Luke Valentine wants to become a BIG TIME illustrator and to work on future titles from the Ms. Ellen's got Swag series. He likes scary movies and videogames and his favorite things to draw are monsters and sneakers.

Made in the USA
Columbia, SC
16 November 2021

48920037R00015